a minedition book

published by Michael Neugebauer Publishing Ltd., Hong Kong
distributed in GB by BOUNCE! Sales and Marketing Ltd, London

Text copyright © 2012 Catherine Leblanc
Illustrations copyright © 2012 Eve Tharlet
English text edited by Martin West
Originally published by Michael Neugebauer Publishing Ltd., Hong Kong.
Rights arranged with "minedition" Rights and Licensing AG, Zurich, Switzerland.
Manufactured in China
Typesetting in Sabon • Colour separation by Hi Fai

A CIP Catalogue record for this book is available from the British Library

ISBN 978-988-15128-0-2

10 9 8 7 6 5 4 3 2 1 First English impression 2011

For more information please visit our website:www.minedition.com

Catherine Leblanc

Will You Still Love Me If ...?

Pictures by Eve Tharlet

minedition

Little Bear tears his jacket when he's playing.
Oh dear, Mum will be angry!

Mum is feeling tired, she's been working all day.
'Oh dear, how did you do that? Give it to me and I'll mend it.'

Little Bear looks sad.
'What's the matter?' Mum asks, as she looks for the right colour thread.
'Mum, I'm sorry I tore my jacket. Do you still love me?'

'Of course I do, why wouldn't I love you,
just because of that?'

As his mum starts to sew with small stitches,
Little Bear rummages through her sewing box.
'If I tore ALL my clothes,
would you still love me?'

'If you did that, I'd be very cross,
but I'd still love you!'

Little Bear feels better.

He's making a house out of all the buttons.
Then he asks:
'If I didn't do any work at school and got
a bad report, would you still love me?'

'I'd be very disappointed but
I would still love you!' says Mum.

'What if I was really naughty and jumped up and down
on my bed and broke it and made a mess in the house,
would you still love me then?'

'I'd be very angry and upset and I would try to
stop you.
But of course I'd still love you!'

Then Little Bear asks a silly question.
'What if I was huge and ugly and green
and covered in bugs?'

'Well, that's different,' laughs Mum.

But Little Bear keeps going.
'You wait, one day you'll stop loving me!'

'Never! You'll always be my Little Bear,
and I'll always love you, no matter what.
That will never change!'

But Little Bear wants to be sure.
'And what if I stopped loving you?'

'Then I would be very, very sad and I would cry,
but I wouldn't stop loving you!'

There is something that still worries
Little Bear very much,
but he doesn't dare ask.
Looking down at the floor and fiddling
with his buttons, at last he asks:
'What if you died?'

His mum stops sewing and looks up.
'That's a difficult question to answer.
But I think that even then I would still love you.'

'But how would I know?' asks Little Bear.

'Well, when you feel the wind gently stroking your fur,
see the stream sparkling in the sunlight,
and when you hear the birds flying above you –
you will know, deep inside.
But I'm still here and I'm not dead yet.'

Little Bear comes over and cuddles close to his mum.

Then suddenly he leaps down and runs around the room.
He runs around faster and faster, making noises like an aeroplane.
'Be quiet, Little Bear!' laughs his mum.
Then Little Bear shouts:
'And what if I don't want you to love me any more?'
Mum looks down at her sewing:
'Oh, I would wait until you loved me again.
It wouldn't take very long …'

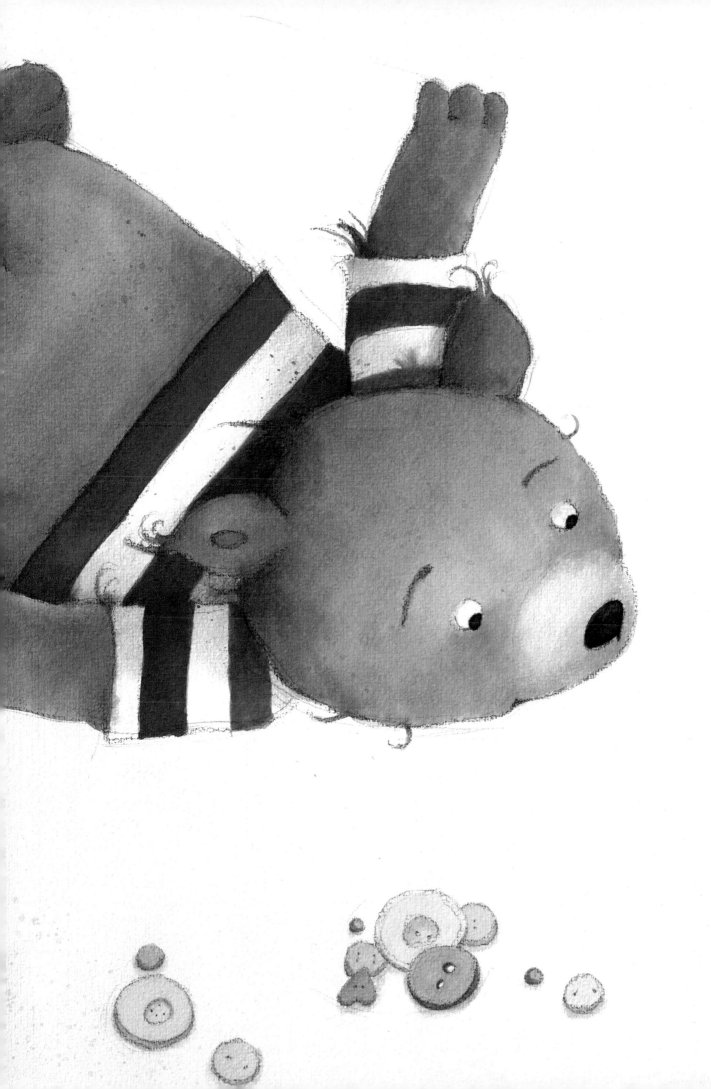

Little Bear looks at her round tummy and asks his last question:
'And what if one day you love someone else more than you love me?'

'More than you? That's impossible!
I might love someone in a different way.
But it wouldn't change anything because I'll always love YOU!'

She ties a knot, bites off the thread and puts his jacket down.
Little Bear pulls it on. He wants to go out to play with his friends.
Then he asks: 'But what if I love somebody else more than I love you?'

Mum looks calmly at Little Bear.
'I will still love you.
You can love whoever you choose.'